Escape From Fate

It Happened in Riverdale, Volume 5

Juliana Harvard

Published by Juliana Harvard, 2021.

ESCAPE FROM FATE

First edition. June 12, 2021.

Copyright © 2021 Juliana Harvard.

ISBN: 979-8201254209

Written by Juliana Harvard.

Table of Contents

To Sandra and Bob for their friendship and support

Chapter 1. Going Separate Ways (Summer 1963)

"WE'LL HAVE FIVE HAMBURGERS and three hot dogs—everything but onions—on the burgers, that is. Oh, yes, make one of those a cheeseburger. And, let's see, how about eight malts—better make two of those shakes. What flavors do you have?"

Sandra groaned to herself as she mechanically threw the meat onto the griddle and splashed the milk and ice cream into the shake maker. At times like this, she wondered why she ever agreed to take this job at Snackies instead of spending a quiet summer doing the sewing she wanted to do for college. College—600 miles away—and Bob! But now there was no time for daydreaming.

When Sandra filled the order, she once again settled down in the empty air-conditioned burger joint. With *her* luck, no one else would be in for even a soda pop for a good hour. Then in sauntered Julie.

"Hi! Been busy?"

"Oh, no," Sandra replied facetiously. "You should have been here ten minutes ago."

Julie laughed. "Hey, how about some water? I'm famished!"

Sandra brought ice water to the short brunette who had already seated herself on a snack bar stool. "You're our best customer—for water, that is! Been shopping?"

"Oh, I just picked up my bedspread and rug at Woolworth's, since *our* plans for rooming together fell through."

"Oh, Julie, don't you think there's *any* more hope? We've planned this for so long! Why should your Momma get cold feet at the last minute? She just wants her little girl—"

"Cut it out, Sandra—it's hard being the youngest child, the last to leave home."

Sandra grinned. "Okay, okay. So you're an only child who's the youngest, and I'm an only child who's the oldest. Honestly, the way Daddy treats me sometimes you'd think I had been born in the Victorian age!"

"Well, at least, you've managed so far to get to be at Emorys' every weekend for the youth socials. And *you* can't complain about that!"

Sandra's eyes sparkled. "Boy, we've sure had some great times over there on Saturday nights—and afternoons, too—haven't we?"

Julie nodded. "It's been a wonderful summer." She stared into the empty glass. With Kurt Gaston and Bill Johnson around, Sandra and Julie hadn't spent one Saturday night at home since that magic weekend last April at Beach City. Now her gaze shifted to Sandra. "What about Bob?"

Vivacious Sandra grew even more restless. "Oh, Julie, I don't know! In a way, I can't wait to get up north at Pacific Christian College with Bob—before it's too late."

"Too late for what?" Julie handed her the empty water glass.

"Julie—I'm falling in love with Kurt. I actually *want* to let him kiss me. And it's not right! It's not fair to Bob—he's waited so long."

"Kurt! But Bill asked you to go steady last—"

"Oh, I know. Julie, honey, I'm sorry. Bill has liked me secretly for a long time—e-even *before* your big quarrel after graduation. He told me never to tell you—it was only a little while after Beach City...."

Julie was silent.

"Julie? Julie, I did everything I could to discourage Bill. He belongs with you. Kurt is so sweet and gentle...." Sandra shook herself. "What am I saying? I belong with Bob!"

Julie smiled. "Don't worry, dear. I don't resent your—your magnetic attractiveness. Anyway, Allen wants to date me again—I don't know why. After the suddenness of that episode at Beach City when he left me for blonde, beautiful Mindi, it's hard to believe he wants me back. And can you blame me for acting like such a fool with the 'marvelous' Bill Johnson that same Saturday night?"

"Julie!" Sandra spoke with playful sternness. "You know good and well—no matter what happened in the past—Allen is in love with you. Always has been, always will be—and is *now!*"

Sandra fetched a glass for herself. "Say, aren't you rather looking forward to staying here in the valley this fall? After all, it's what, eight miles, from Macintoshes' new house in Oak Grove to La Paloma College?"

"But Allen will be almost a hundred miles from La Paloma after school starts when he goes back to San Margo Academy for his senior year." It was an attempted matter-of-fact reply.

"But there'll be plenty of opportunities for you to get away from La Paloma and, of course, he'll be coming home now and then—"

"Sandra, I want to go to Pacific Christian College as badly as you do!"

Silently, Sandra set down her glass then leaned on the counter, her chin in her hands and her eyes fastened on Julie.

Julie stood up. "W-well, *almost* as badly as you do. See you!"

Sandra laughed as Julie's well-rounded figure slipped out the door and into her car. She returned the bewitching grin before Julie put on her glasses and drove away. Then the long shining hair behind the steering wheel disappeared as Julie's Rambler disappeared in traffic.

Sandra could see her reflection in Snackies' window. *My magnetic attractiveness?* She giggled to herself. *I'm a scrawny red-faced college freshman who most people mistake for age 13 or 14, with beady eyes peering from under coarse, slightly auburn, piled-on-top-of-the-head hair, which I seldom can manage.* Turning from the window, she shrugged. *If Bill wanted to go steady with me, and Kurt wants to kiss me, if Bob is in love with me, and Daddy thinks I'm Victorian—and Julie envies me—who cares?!*

Chapter 2. In Their Own Worlds (Fall 1963)

THE WEEKS PASSED QUICKLY, bringing the late-summer heat wave, then the falling leaves. And it put 600 miles between two girls who had been best friends since fifth grade.

"...and I had only been on campus ten days before my first date with Glen! Boy, this weekend in the mountains is just too much for words—I never knew a pre-med could be so exciting..." Sandra chuckled out loud.

"What is it, roommate?"

"Oh, Anna, it's just a letter from my friend at home, Julie Scott. It's only October, but it sounds like she's really having a ball. No," she muttered half to herself, "I don't need to worry about her. I just hope things will work out for Bob and me."

"...but the very night Glen decided physics was more important than romance, Larry appeared and took me to the concert..."

"...I thought the phone call was really something, then when he sent the flowers for my birthday, I could hardly believe it. Sandra, do you think maybe Allen really does still like me?"

"...Imagine Kurt and Bill coming over to see me! But I guess they do miss us—but especially you. They asked about you..."

Sandra hesitated to pick up the pen. Slowly she wrote, "Dear Julie, I guess you're having a great time down there, aren't you? Oh, I'm so mixed up I don't know what to do! Bob wants to get married next summer, and I'm not even sure I'm in love with him. No, it's not Kurt or Bill—I just don't know. We've had some great times together—he does everything he can for me—I just don't have the feelings I should have. I want to love him, really

I do, but I hardly know him—we've been apart so long. And what should I take for my major? Daddy's always plugged for the teacher idea, but I want to be a social worker—or maybe even Bob's wife..."

And Julie wrote back. *"...and, Sandra, I've met the most wonderful man in the world! His name is Mike Kirwin and he rides a motorcycle. Besides being another pre-med and terribly admiring, he's such a good Christian and wants to be a missionary. Man, I can sure understand now about your flings when you were away from Bob. Kid, what if Mike and Allen both come to see me during vacation? What a neat situation! (Ha!) By the way, things will work out for you and Bob. He's loved you deeply for over two years—even when he was supposedly dating me. Anyway, your decision about a major will come, too; magically, someday you'll know exactly what you want..."*

Sandra smiled to herself as she checked the date on Julie's last letter. She started it two weeks ago. If Julie only knew now just how things were working out.

"HONEY, YOU DON'T KNOW how happy it makes me to hear you say it," Bob breathed as he lingered en route from Nelson Library to the girls' dorm.

"Well, I *do* love you," Sandra responded, "like I've never loved any other boy before in my life."

Bob touched her hand. "Mrs. Bob Miller," he whispered. "Someday, someday."

The Christmas spirit permeated the air the day Sandra packed and said goodbye to Bob. "I sure wish you were going back to Riverdale with me, honey."

"Well, princess, I do, too. But, well, we need the money. We both have debts to pay off. Now you be good while you're home! And, merry Christmas, sweetheart!"

Sandra returned his kiss and got onto the plane. As the silver machine soared through the clouds, she knew this vacation would be the actual test of her love for Bob—when she would be around Kurt and Bill once more.

Chapter 3. Christmas Vacation in Riverdale (Winter 1963)

"OH, JULIE, LONG TIME no see! Let's get together and have a nice long talk—you must tell me all about Mike Kirwin—"

"Well, uh, I think Mike and I are about through—my Momma, well, you know how she is. Say, how about you and me and Allen and Kurt going caroling Christmas Eve?"

"Well, I don't know. Bob—"

"They've already planned it. Bill's in L.A. and won't be here in Riverdale until Christmas Day. Hey, what's this about Bob?"

"Oh, Julie, Daddy just brought the car home—I'll be right over!"

Sandra found one merry girl sitting by the tree and an admiring Allen looking on as she opened his gift. Unnoticed, Sandra stood by the door as Allen and Julie shared a soft, sweet Christmas kiss. There was no need to even ask about Mike anymore!

"Sandra! Come on in," called Julie. "Hey, how about tonight?"

"Kurt would sure like to see you," Allen winked.

"We-l-l—" Sandra blushed slightly.

"Come on, I'll call him and tell him you're here." Julie rose to her feet and grabbed the phone. Sandra started to protest—but didn't.

Soon Kurt and Sandra and Allen and Julie were on their way to the church to pick up a couple of carol books. But their caroling trip got no farther. By the time they had agreed on what carols to use, what parts each would sing, and so on, the hands of the chapel clock had almost reached ten. They all went back to Julie's house.

"So long!" Allen called as Kurt pulled out from Julie's driveway. Then he turned to Julie.

"Well, sweetheart, I'll see you New Year's Eve." Allen kissed her lips gently.

"A-hem!" Sandra teasingly cleared her throat loudly.

Julie sighed softly as Allen's car, too, disappeared into the darkness. "Have fun tonight, Sandra?"

"Huh?" Sandra started from her daydreaming. "Oh, yeah, I guess so. I, uh, see you and Allen are, uh—"

"Oh, Sandra," Julie drooled, "it's really neat now!"

Sandra beamed. "I know. I'm really in love with Bob. Last summer—" She laughed and shook her head. "Kurt and Bill are just boys. It was just a summer fling. You know, Julie, tonight was really boring with Kurt. I mean, I *like* Kurt; but I *love* Bob. I'm sure of it now."

"I'm happy for you," Julie reflected as she remembered Sandra's many past dilemmas with romance. Every fellow had literally swept Sandra off her feet, but somehow never quite seemed to fill the place in Sandra's heart. Julie was sure this time, Bob would fill that place.

"Mrs. Allen Macintosh," Sandra teased. "Well, I'll see you spring vacation—if I can tear myself away from Bob for five days!"

"Okay, Mrs. Miller," Julie returned. "Be sure to write!"

Julie and Sandra waved goodbye as long as they could see each other. Then, once again, the two girls went their separate ways.

"...and we don't know what we're going to do," Sandra wrote. *"Bob doesn't have a cent to his name besides what he's working for here. We both don't really want to borrow more money for school next year. It's been pretty hard since Mom died—especially for Daddy. He'll never let me get married if he's still alone. If only Bob and I could get a married couples' cottage at La Paloma next year, but there's still the problem of getting Bob to leave the North Country that he loves so much. And he would have to transfer from a*

quarter system college to a semester system. We want to get married as soon as possible, but it's so hard to be good..."

Be good... Julie smiled a little as she answered Sandra's letter. *"...but love is good; love is sacred—and very, very special. Sandra, I'm in love, too. I love Allen so much deeper than I've ever loved any other man—and more than I ever could love another. Something very wonderful has happened to us..."*

"Sandra! I'm speaking to you!" Anna nudged her again.

"Huh? Oh." Sandra looked up from Julie's letter. "Sorry, roommate."

"Who is your girlfriend Julie rooming with at La Paloma?"

"A girl named Bobbie Crawford, I think she told me."

Anna gasped. "You're kidding! I knew her from Highview."

"What's she like?" Sandra was a little cautious.

"I didn't know her too well," Anna drawled. "Last I saw her—several months ago—she was dating quite a Romeo, Derek somebody. Oh, Bobbie's okay—I just didn't expect your best girlfriend to be rooming with her." Anna shrugged.

Sandra's thoughts lingered. *"Love...special...something happened to us—"* No! she thought. *Julie's a good kid. Forget it, Sandra Lee!*

BOB'S SLIGHT FRAME sank wearily into the velvety parlor sofa as he smiled sleepily into Sandra's sparkling eyes. "Aw, honey, I'm sorry I don't feel like taking you to the Valentine party. You understand?"

"Sure I do," Sandra soothed him. "You work *too* hard, honey. I really pray hard that we'll make it through another year and a half. Your diploma means a lot, I know."

"But *what* to get a degree in!" Bob almost winced. "Theology—but there's that Greek. Besides, it would mean two more years at the seminary—more money, more bills. Yet, everyone frowns on me giving up the ministry for a career in electronics engineering or computer science. I want to take care of you when I marry you, and I want to marry you soon!"

"Well, I can't marry *anybody* until I graduate from college, so Daddy says. Where's the money coming from? Besides, I'm not even sure what I'm going to major in."

Bob patted her hand as he managed a weak smile. "Honey, it takes a lot of faith—and prayers."

Sandra sighed. "You're so right, Bob."

Chapter 4. Spring Break (Spring 1964)

AS SANDRA WANDERED down the silent dormitory hall in search of Julie, she was not a little reminiscent of the year she had spent at La Paloma away from Bob. The basement wing where Julie was now—that was where Sandra had lived, too, until her mother had taken sick and the tragedy struck. Life had seemed like one dreadful nightmare. She remembered the sickening white of the hospital walls and the morning fog that smothered the valley and the La Paloma campus. The organ, the black clothes and green carpets, the smell of oak and roses all spun around Sandra's tear-stained face—then Bob was there. Yes, things had looked pretty dark then. So slowly the wound had healed. Now Daddy had a girlfriend—Sandra hoped—and at least Bob still loved her, very much....

"Sandra! What are you doing here?" It was the familiar sound of Julie's voice.

"Oh, hi! I was just coming down to see you, Julie," Sandra greeted her friend. "Too bad our Easter vacations didn't coincide. But I thought I'd stop in and see you before I go back to Pacific."

"Well, I'm glad you did. Come on down to my room and we can catch up on all the gossip. Bobbie's out tonight."

And so, after almost an hour of Julie's study time had slipped away, Sandra bade her friend goodbye.

"See you next summer—I hope!" Sandra said.

"You *hope!*" Julie questioned. "Aren't you and Bob going to spend the summer in Riverdale?"

"I don't know," Sandra replied. "He's got a good year-round job at Pacific Christian College—even if he does nearly work himself to death. And Daddy has talked about getting me a neat office job with some friend of his in town. But how can Bob and I spend another summer apart? Last summer was enough!" Then Sandra grinned. "But, no need to worry. We both know, 'all things work together for good'..."

Julie smiled as Sandra waved goodbye and hopped into the taxi. She was so optimistic. That was just Sandra.

"AND HOW'S 'LITTLE SIS'?" Bob asked.

Sandra opened her mouth to ask "who" but only for a moment. Julie, of course! Making her his "little sister" had been Bob's way of trying hard to not hurt her when he had fallen in love with Sandra. "Oh, just fine, I guess," Sandra responded.

"Is she still in love with Allen?" he asked teasingly.

Sandra's expression remained unusually serious.

"Confidentially, honey, I'm just a little worried. Julie and I had a nice long talk—about Allen. They're in love, all right, but—"

Bob's smile faded. "But Julie's too sweet for Allen to hurt her—again."

"Really," Sandra went on, "I thought we were bad that Saturday night at Willow Creek. But Julie and Allen don't even believe it's wrong!"

"Willow Creek." Bob's worry showed as he remorsefully remembered that night. "But how could they ever—"

"Well, it seems one night they got off campus with Bobbie and Derek. Remember that place called Rainbow Rock on that little road north of La Paloma College? I know you've heard about it—"

Bob took her hand. "Say no more, sweetheart. Just pray that Julie's still a virgin."

THE CAMPUS WAS A WORLD of springtime colors and activities. The springtime whirl caught both Sandra and Julie—even in their two separate worlds.

"But I just couldn't go out on Derek the way you go out on Allen," Bobbie insisted. "Sometimes I wonder if you really are in love."

"Oh, good grief!" Julie protested. "Of course, I love Allen. It's just that he's there and Rafael's here. I think you're just like my Momma—objecting to Rafael Gonzales just because he's Spanish!"

"No, I'm not," Bobbie argued. "Allen may not be the handsomest man in the world, but Rafael sure isn't!"

"That's not true!" defended Julie. "Rafael's really cute. Anyway, he's nice, too. But you know I'm going to marry Allen!"

Bobbie nodded, then lowered her eyebrows slightly. "Julie, aren't you really rebelling? Going out with Rafael just because your Momma is a little prejudiced. Protesting against what you've believed all your life?"

Julie was silent. It was hopeless to argue with Bobbie.

"RAFAEL GONZALES, HUH?" Bob asked Sandra.

"Um-hum." Sandra absentmindedly stuffed Julie's letter back into its envelope.

"Well, maybe more casual dating of other guys will make Julie a little more inhibited when she's out with Allen alone."

"Yeah, maybe." Sandra was now leafing through her notebook. Then, "Hey, we've got two minutes to get to English Lit—let's go!" And Bob followed her racing feet out the dormitory door.

"...SO IF BOB CAN STAY in the trailer in your yard like he did two summers ago, we'll be in Riverdale for the summer and maybe go to La Paloma College this fall. I've got a 50-50 chance for a library job, but Bob is coming completely on faith. Oh, Julie, you're so lucky! You're so positive of your secretarial ambitions and you have your California State Scholarship to put you through your four years. And then you'll have Allen for a lifetime. 'Pastor and Mrs. Allen Macintosh.' Bob is so torn, but we can't get married until he graduates with something and has a job!"

Julie plopped onto the bed and dropped Sandra's letter on her desk. With chin in hands and pensive eyes gazing far across the warm green campus, she reaffirmed silently how happy—and lucky—she really was. Allen was hers, all hers, and she was his. How could Sandra possibly understand how much she had grown since Christmas! Bob was so much more warmly emotional than Allen that, of course, he and Sandra had to be careful. But Allen was levelheaded—and so lovingly affectionate. No, not even Bobbie Crawford really understood their unique relationship, the tangible and intangible things that bound their hearts together....

Chapter 5. Back in Riverdale (Early June 1964)

"OH! YOU'RE *really* here!" It was plain to see that Julie was excited as she gave Bob a quick once-over.

Sandra hugged Bob. "Yep, all summer! Then one more year together—most likely at La Paloma—and then..." Her eyes spelled "wedding bells."

"Neat!" Julie agreed. "Well, I guess you know I'll be staying at La Paloma for summer school until August."

"But after August, you're really going to live it up," Bob directed to Julie as he hugged Sandra. "Allen and I are going to show you gals the works—mountains, beach, Disneyland—"

Julie giggled. "Well, don't forget to tell Allen about it."

"Say," reminded Sandra, "Allen's down south working for that evangelism scholarship, isn't he?"

Julie nodded. "Just eight more weeks! Then we'll be together—a little summer, then college, then a lifetime."

THE NEXT COUPLE OF weeks were busy ones. Allen, just a little unsure of his long-desired plans for the ministry, was eager to get involved in this little taste of real evangelism, even if it meant more than a hundred miles away from his Julie. Although she was feeling alone, Julie soon lost herself in the whirl of the Western Civilization summer class and her job at La Paloma. Sandra, energetic and happy to be free from finals, soon landed a neat little position in the city library. And

Bob, worn down but not out from hunting a job, satisfied himself with a temporary job at the Riverdale Packing Company while he looked for something—anything—that was better.

"Well," Julie admitted to Sandra, "Larry and Glen both asked me if I'd play tennis with them this summer, but I haven't seen either around." She shrugged as she stared out Bob's trailer door. "And I miss my 'good buddy.'"

"Rafael?" Bob ventured a guess.

"No, I mean Greg Schultz," Julie smiled. "I told you two about him. He's in my music theory class, but what he'd *really* like to do is theater. We were so close, like brother and sister. He took me to the Spring Banquet at Mission Inn, but he can't afford to come back to La Paloma."

"He must have needed a Christian friend like you," Bob nodded.

"But, speaking of Rafael—" Julie eyed Bob and Sandra mischievously as she dug into her purse and produced a small airmail envelope. "I heard from him last week."

"Wow!" Sandra exclaimed as she looked at the letter Julie held in her hand.

"Oh, but it's not what you think," Julie explained. "It's a goodbye letter. He's spending the summer working at a hospital in Ohio."

Sandra frowned, but Julie went on.

"I didn't even *like* Rafael when I first started dating him. I just went with him to all those Spanish-speaking churches to play the piano for him when he sang. But we spent a lot of time together rehearsing in the music building practice rooms. And, well, after a while, before I knew what was happening, we were falling in love." She stopped for a moment, remembering, as a smile played on her lips. Then, returning to the moment, she said, "Here's what Rafael wrote in this letter." And Julie read, "Juliana, you are the first woman I've ever been in love with; and I know that if I ever fall in love again, it will have to be with someone who is as wonderful as you."

"Wow!" Sandra didn't know what else to say.

IT WAS LATER WHEN SANDRA and Julie were alone that Sandra remembered something she had heard. "Say, I didn't know your Aunt Jenny passed away."

"Oh," Julie responded a little sadly, "yes. It was just before finals last spring and I had to come home for five days. She and Momma were so close. It terrified me to go back, but I made it okay."

"I'm sorry." Sandra's eyes wandered far beyond the sunflowers just outside Julie's bedroom window. "I remember when my Aunt Hazel died a couple years ago. My mother was the one who took such constant care of her when she was so sick. You know, no one would have ever dreamed then that my mother would go so soon afterwards."

Suddenly a strange new pang of fear shot through Julie's body like no sensation she had ever felt before. Trembling, she left the room. "Sandra," she called over her shoulder, "let's play the piano—or something."

Chapter 6. Summer Fun Times (Mid-June 1964)

"KURT! BILL! HEY, YOU guys, quit fooling around!" Sandra directed this to the pile of rocks on the little knoll where her two young friends were mischievously trying to sneak around the other side.

Bob, just out of breath from jumping across the rocks, landed beside Sandra and gave her a quick squeeze. Then he added, "Okay, you two, we can see your heads bobbing around back there!"

Meanwhile, Bob's pretend little "sisters" Julie and Darlene had walked across the field from the farmhouse. Now Julie joined in with, "Come on, you guys!" Darlene just giggled.

In a moment, Kurt, the younger one, walked nonchalantly from around the north end of the biggest rock. "Have you people seen Bill?" he asked in fake innocence.

Just then a tall lanky figure sprang from his precarious position on a higher rock, crashed through the dry leaves, and bounded down the hill. He laughed. "I almost slipped!"

This was the summer home for 16-year-old Darlene, the youngest of the group. Although Darlene had spent the day in town with the rest of the gang, her big "sister" Julie had brought her back to Harvey Hills Ranch for another week's work. Now the six of them gathered on the flat rock at the base of the live oak tree whose dark green branches created silhouettes in the pale hazy sky. Far across the parched field, the jagged purple mountains rose, hiding the softly fading gold and crimson that streaked the June sky. Not even a breeze was astir as the most welcome coolness settled over the warm earth. Julie, especially, gazed into the sunset. And there was silence.

After their quiet evening worship prayer of thankfulness, it was a long moment before anyone could speak. Then magically their voices united in a simple hymn as the stars appeared like little lights in the window of heaven. The cowbells rang in the distance. Soon, with their "moo's" piercing the stillness, the cows ambled their dark bodies along the dirt road and broke through the twilighted grayness where the sunset had been only minutes before.

The kids climbed into Julie's car, Darlene got off at the farmhouse farther up the road, and the rest went back to Riverdale to Julie's place. They all involved themselves in playful teasing and lively chatter.

IT WAS WELL PAST MIDNIGHT when Bill and Kurt, who Julie had been entertaining, finally decided it was time to go home. Bob would take Sandra home later. For a long time, Julie curled up in Grandpa Philip's big chair and watched her "big brother" and her best friend who sat on the sofa. It made her think of herself and Allen. Allen! She thought of Allen mostly, unless she spent her time with Bill and Kurt—or Darlene or Bob and Sandra—or maybe school.

"Just think, Julie, this time next week!" It was Sandra who spoke.

"Allen will be here?" Bob was thinking about Allen, too. This was the chance Julie had waited for.

"How should I know?" she growled. "*You* read the letter."

"Little sis," Bob sighed, "we've gone through all this so many times." Turning to Sandra, he said, "Weren't you two making plans for next weekend?"

Sandra was enthusiastic. "Oh, yes! We thought Allen could stay with you in the trailer either Friday or Saturday night, depending on when he has to go back. Then on the Fourth of July, we can all four visit with his parents in Oak Grove and come back about five for Julie's mother's surprise birthday dinner. Then we'll go to the swimming party at Donaldsons' on Saturday night." Sandra went on until Julie, too, had caught the spirit.

"Fine, fine!" Bob agreed when the girls had given all the details. "It sounds great—a real ball!"

Sandra grinned. "Isn't it neat to be in love?"

"I guess so," Julie shrugged, looking just a little puzzled.

"What's the matter, sis?" asked Bob, noticing a slight cloud that only he would notice. "Aren't you *really* in love with Allen?"

"Why, sure," Julie said lightly, her cynical arrogance turned on. "But, man, that has nothing to do with it! Remember last summer—"

Sandra shut her eyes. "I'd really rather not." They both remembered it well. "Oh, Julie," she continued, "my entire world has changed so completely since then. Sure, I'll admit we never had a dull Saturday night from April to September, and Bob being 600 miles away at Pacific Christian College wasn't much more than a dream to rely on when no one else was around. But something happened to us, Julie. Bob and I fell in love—genuine love..." Bob fastened his eyes on Sandra.

"Aw, but now you're 'tied down'—no offense, brother dear—and I've got a brilliant career ahead—executive secretary, seeing the world, traveling—"

Sandra's voice was tender. "Oh, Julie, being a wife, a mother—especially when you've got a great guy like Bob—it's the greatest career any girl could have! That's the way God meant it to be. Sure, you can work after marriage if you want to. But you've got something much better than an empty apartment to come home to. You've got a wonderful husband, and all the love in the entire universe is yours."

Julie was silent for a long moment. Then, in a more settled voice, she said, "Okay, I know you're sold on the marriage and family idea. I guess I can't help but agree; I really do plan to get married someday. But this summer"—she winked at Sandra—"it won't be too hard for Darlene and me to get with Kurt and Bill!"

Bob lowered his eyebrows. "And you plan to settle down to Allen when your little fling's all over with?"

"Why not?" Julie was strangely flippant.

"Are you sure Allen really loves you?" Bob asked pointedly.

Now Julie's artificial carelessness changed to genuine concern. "I don't know, Bob. I want to believe we're in love, really I do. Just because he dated a few girls when he was away at school at San Margo Academy—"

"A few!" retorted Sandra. "Eleven girls just since Christmas?"

"Well, I dated, too." Julie was quick to reply.

"Three or four guys," Bob reminded. "And each one of those relationships came from a deep Christian sense of caring for them as people who needed what you, as a Christian sister, could give."

Julie's eyes dropped, though she pretended to ignore the observation. "I don't want to believe all those stories Cynthia Donaldson has been telling me. She goes to school with him at San Margo Academy. She knows what he does, what the 'good kids' think of him. Oh, Bob! How could I believe we would grow away from each other! After almost four years—" Julie buried her face.

"That's what I'm afraid is happening, little sis." Bob's voice was characteristically kind. "Unless some grand miracle comes."

"The miracle of love?" Julie looked up.

Bob almost smiled through his unusual seriousness. "If you're patient—if you *really* love him—if you wait until he grows up, if you understand him, think with him, feel with him—if it's really God's will—you will."

"I think I want to." Julie dropped onto the bearskin rug at the end of the Victorian sofa. "But I don't know what to say, what to talk about when I'm with him. All he ever talks about—if it isn't love-talk to me—is all the petty pranks he and his roommate pull. And the serious talks seem so superficial. I've got a new vision of life. When his dad was the pastor here in Riverdale, he had quite a lot to do with it. And I want to share this happiness with Allen. I want us to understand each other and communicate—besides being able to have such fabulous times together. I'd like to help him if I could and should, but I *don't* want to sound like his father!"

"By *all* means, don't!" Bob echoed. His understanding smile faded slowly as he said, "Only Love itself can tell you what to do."

"But if we don't love each other, we must break up eventually, won't we?" Julie seemed almost helpless.

"Well, if you do break up, make it final," Bob advised, thinking back over the rocky past Julie had had with Allen. "Leave absolutely no glimmer of hope—it'll only make it more painful for both of you."

"But what if there *is* hope, later—much later? Say in about five years!" Julie almost chuckled at her self-made cliché.

"That's the future and it'll take care of itself. For *now,* if you break up—if you should—you must forget everything."

"Oh, but the very thought of breaking up! It's been so long, and after all we've done and gone through—together. And when we're together, I feel *sure* we love each other. How could I, after we've had a neat time next Saturday night, just say, 'Well, Allen, I guess this is it—goodbye'? It can't be that simple!"

"It's hard, I know," Bob said, "but that's the way life is. I don't know; maybe you *do* love him—even if he doesn't become a minister like you've always dreamed."

"Oh, Bob"—and he knew by her tone that he had pushed a button—"just so long as we both love God. I'm all for whatever he wants to do, whatever will make him happiest. But I just want him to be *something.* He has to wake up one of these days soon—he'll be a college man in a few months!—and realize it's time to grow up and start thinking and living in the adult world. I'm sure it's only adolescent confusion. Despite his grades, I *know* he's very intelligent! He'll find himself—and his God. He *will* grow up, Bob; after all, we're only seventeen!"

"Then," breathed Bob, studying the pattern on the Indian vase that sat on the antique end table, "be patient—wait. But never let him *know* you're waiting—that's for his mother to do. He must feel you're growing *with* him—and you must."

"Bob?" Her expression reminded Sandra of the time they were lost in Los Angeles when they were only nine. "What if—what if we *don't*...grow...together?"

"Are you really afraid, sis?"

Julie could not reply.

Bob stroked the long dark hair that fell softly on her crumpled shoulder. "I—we—love you, sis, very much. God has *someone* for you to love and to love you—like Sandra and me." He kissed her forehead lightly. "Maybe it's Allen—maybe not. But it isn't right for you to live in fear, plagued with doubts, frustrated by what's supposed to be love. Sis, it's up to you—and Allen."

Julie tore at her fingernails for a moment. "Bob—" But as she looked up, her words faded to the kiss that Bob and Sandra were sharing. She watched them—this time, not in reminiscence, but in pain. It was not because it was a mere kiss, but because of all the things it symbolized—love, genuine love, marriage, a home blessed by God. She rose slowly and tiptoed to her room.

"Goodnight, sis," Bob called quietly as she shut the door behind her.

THE MORNING DAWNED just a little misty. When Julie finally got up, Bob was not in his trailer. Oh, yes, she remembered, Bob and Sandra had left early to go to the beach. Mechanically, she straightened her room and packed the suitcase to go back to summer school at La Paloma College for another week.

After a home-cooked breakfast with the family—except for Bob and Darlene—Julie had a few hours of world history to go through. With heart and soul, Julie plunged into the revolutions of the 1820s and 1830s until the sun was high in the sky. Then she put her books and suitcase into the Rambler.

"Bye, now; be careful, hon!" Those were always Momma's last words as she kissed her before she started back. Julie backed the car down the long unpaved driveway, then stopped to shut the gate.

But she stood at the gate longer than usual this time, her hand resting on the iron latch, and stared toward the house. There it stood, in their modernized neighborhood, in all of its two-story colonial splendor. It wasn't really such a big or fancy house, and its wooden exterior was obviously in need of a little paint. The lazy elms that shaded almost the whole sparsely grass-covered yard seemed to sigh in memory with her. There, in the place where her cardboard playhouse used to stand, was the recent addition of Bob's trailer for the summer. His "home" would soon mean him and Sandra.

Momma and Grandpa had just come out of the house to sit under the trees and share cool lemonade. Julie, unnoticed by them, wondered what life had been like a generation ago. Momma had grown up in this same house. *I wonder if she had close friends like I have Sandra and Darlene—friends who seem like sisters to me? Did she have a "big brother" like Bob to give her endless advice on love and stuff?* But soon the hour-long drive back to La Paloma College that afternoon took Julie back into the new world of academia she had so recently discovered.

For five more days there was the familiar routine—working as secretary at the Institute of Health every morning, history class with the beloved Dr. Mackey, afternoons and evenings devoted to untiring study as she bravely struggled with the Greeks for independence, triumphed with the founders of the Second French Republic, and amused herself with *Communist Manifesto* excerpts. Then, twice a week, there were the worships in the lovely little chapel across the campus. Only at night came the slightly heartsick pangs as she read from the lovely white Bible that Allen had given her on the very first Christmas they had shared, and as she looked at his lifelike picture that stood prominently on the end of her desk by the lamp....

Chapter 7. A Summer Storm (Late June 1964)

WHEN THE END OF THE week came, Julie packed her suitcase for another weekend, cleaned her room, flicked the light switch, and locked the door. She stopped briefly at the gas station. And then—home! The miles could not go by fast enough. Before turning into the welcome driveway, Julie stopped for the mail. There was Bob's paycheck, Momma's new flower catalog, a card from Darlene—and a letter from Allen.

"Yes, sweetheart, I'll be down for the Fourth," it said. "Your plans sound swell. Maybe Mom and Dad will come to your place for the dinner, too. And a swimming party at Donaldsons' sounds wonderful! We'll go to the beach next time I'm home. Tell Bob thanks for his invitation—I think I can stay Saturday night with him at your place, unless something drastic happens (ha! ha!). I love you...."

Julie stuffed the letter back into its envelope and hurried on into the house.

Bob's ready smile was there to greet her. "How was your week, sis? Sorry, I have to run now, but I've got to pick up Sandra. Maybe I'll bring her back here for supper." And once again Julie was spinning in her old familiar world.

Plans could not have worked out any more perfectly than they did that weekend. Bob and Sandra, just bursting to announce their engagement, were most eager and happy to talk to Pastor Don and Betty Macintosh—Allen's parents. And Momma's surprise birthday dinner worked like a charm! She couldn't have suspected it less. Then the screams and laughter from the pool at Donaldsons' drowned any gloominess that might have crept into the hot summer day. There were the usual soda floats to top everything off—then Allen was the first to see the clouds.

Bob, Sandra, Allen, and Julie had said goodbye to the gang and made their way to Bob's car when Sandra suddenly remembered she still had Kurt's car keys, which she had playfully confiscated during the pool party. Kurt and Bill, of course, were still in the pool trying to outdo each other in endurance. Bob and Sandra went back to take Kurt's keys to him. Allen and Julie stood outside by the car.

"Where's the moon tonight?" asked Allen mystically.

Julie looked up into the darkened, starless sky. "Guess there isn't any moon tonight," she concluded casually.

"But there was an almost full moon last night," Allen persisted. "It's the clouds—see? See that faint patch of light behind the power lines—that's the moon behind the clouds."

"Oh." Julie wasn't particularly concerned with moon or clouds.

"There's going to be an unexpected storm tonight," Allen went on. "Wait and see."

"Hey, when did you become Mr. Weatherman?" Julie teased.

But Allen was dead serious. "Don't be surprised at anything that happens tonight, Julie. Most people wouldn't expect it, but—"

But Bob and Sandra had returned, laughing and loving and living in their own special way. Allen opened the car door and he and Julie got inside.

They were almost home when it started to rain, large splashy drops, at first, that plopped like little fat people on the windshield. Julie put her hand out the open window. The raindrops felt warm and wet—almost like teardrops.

"Say, I guess you were right!" Julie directed to Allen. "But it's probably only a summer shower. It won't last too long."

"It may last," Allen disputed in that same low ghostly voice, "quite a while."

"Wh-what?" For the first time in months, Julie was afraid of Allen as she looked questioningly into his emotionless eyes.

"Hey, you two," Bob called from a seemingly different world, "what do you want to do tomorrow? What time do you have to be back, Allen?"

Allen answered, but Julie did not hear. The sound of impending doom was ringing in her ears.

The rain was growing worse and worse until, by the time the kids got home, they were glad for the shelter of the ancient house. It had even thundered just before they shut the door behind them. Just then, there was a knock at the door.

"Darlene!" Julie exclaimed. "Don't knock; come on in!"

"Well," Darlene drawled, "I didn't want to bother anyone. I mean, well, you four—well, anyway—"

Darlene's characteristic blush made Julie laugh. "You're staying in town for the night, aren't you?" Julie guessed. "It's raining pretty hard now to go back."

"Oh, it's not that," insisted Darlene. "Just that the dirt roads out at Harvey Hills get pretty muddy—"

"Don't make excuses." Julie pulled her inside.

"Well, if you don't mind," Darlene said hurriedly, "I think I'll go straight to bed. I'm pretty tired."

Julie, seeing Darlene's slight glance at the four of them, protested when Bob said, "But won't you join us for some hot chocolate and popcorn?"

"Are you kidding!" Darlene groaned and put both hands on her stomach. "After all the food we had at Donaldsons'?"

"Well, some popcorn, anyway." Bob winked, knowing Darlene's secret passion for hot buttered popcorn on rainy nights.

Darlene followed them into the kitchen and became engrossed in popcorn making and gay patter with Bob and Sandra, while Allen and

Julie stood silently side by side and watched the rain beat upon the sullen earth.

"Funny," Allen grunted. "This time last week I would never have guessed."

"Neither would I." Julie did not even raise her eyes.

"Well, it's been a good summer—" The strangeness in Allen's voice was almost unnoticed—"a good romance."

Allen's voice showed no inflections. "Don't deny it, Julie. We were both at that party tonight. I know what they've been saying—I know how you feel."

"But I've told no one how I feel!" She stopped quickly, fearing self-exposure.

"Just your dear best friend and your trustworthy 'brother,'" he said. "But," he interjected as she protested, "nobody said anything to me. I know—I knew it."

Julie was quiet only a moment. "But does it *have* to happen, Allen? This storm, the rain, the tortured silence?"

"I still love you, Julie," he replied like a true philosopher, "in my own boyish way. But you're a woman now. How can you wait for me?"

"How can I *not* wait?" Julie was growing weak.

"Please don't get sentimental," he said, not unkindly. "I know there's no more hope, not now, not for a long time—maybe never."

"Five years?" But Julie's struggling attempt at humor failed.

"Maybe five hundred. Whenever I grow up, whenever I find myself—in your adult world. But maybe we'll still be in different worlds—maybe not. No one can say until the time comes—if it ever does."

"Oh, Allen, please—"

"Popcorn and chocolate's ready!" called Sandra cheerfully.

"Come on," Allen nudged.

Reluctantly, Julie went. Amidst the conversation, she was hardly aware of when Darlene bounded away with, "Night, sis; I'm going to bed. Don't wake me up when you crawl in!"

Julie suddenly noticed the faded gray and white tile squares on the kitchen floor. She remembered when she had scattered that floor with her paper dolls or chalked up with hopscotch. Just a few feet over there was the thin blue Persian rug that stretched almost wall-to-wall across the living room floor. But she mustn't live in the past—there must be a clean break. There had to be—

"Oh, uh, let's go on into the living room and turn on the hi-fi." Julie knew the others were watching her. But they had just gotten settled when the music stopped and the lights went out.

Sandra, as expected, squealed with, "Oooh, Bob, I'm afraid of the dark!"

"I'll hold your hand, little girl," Bob returned.

Julie's quick efficiency soon produced a storm candle she set on the iron chest at the opposite end of the sofa. The light revealed Bob and Sandra's usual embrace and kiss. Julie giggled.

Julie noted it was at this very time a week before when Bob and Sandra had sat in the same spot. But this time, instead of being curled up alone in Grandpa's chair, Julie sat with Allen on the other end of the sofa. The storm showed little sign of letting up. Both Allen and Julie wished that the power line to the house hadn't broken when the eucalyptus limb fell; now they couldn't even have any soft spooky music to set the scene.

Allen turned his face toward Julie's, but she pulled away just before his lips touched hers. Slowly Allen withdrew his arm that had rested on her shoulder.

The candlelight's flickering was casting weird shadows around the room as the wind howled mournfully outside and dashed the water against the old windowpanes. And the rain was still falling fast and hard.

She knew the time had come. But she knew better than to make plans for Bill. As handsome and brawny as Bill might be, he was still in love with Sandra—Bob or no Bob. Besides, there was that cute new girl Beth; even Sandra had hinted that there might be something there as far as Bill was concerned.

As for Kurt, well, he was pretty special. But not even Julie could quite match up to Kurt's intellectual world. And guys at school—there was no hope there until September. Two and a half long hot dreary months lay ahead. Julie knew the score well.

Now the wind had ceased; only the monotonous pitter-pitter-patter-splash continued in the night. Allen placed one hand on Julie's hands, folded in her lap. It reminded her of a November night long, long ago—almost four years now—their very first date when he had first held her hand. Now he took her chin in his other hand and pressed her trembling lips close to his own.

"Allen." Her voice reflected all the simplicity and wide-eyed romance that it had held that November night.

"Julie." It was automatic.

She chuckled, thinking of a corny television commercial for shortening. "Snowdrift!"

His face was expressionless.

BOB ROSE SLOWLY AND stretched, then he gently pulled Sandra to her feet. "About time to go home, angel?"

Sandra nodded. "If we're going to Disneyland tomorrow."

He kissed her cheek lightly.

"Well, Julie, if I don't see you tomorrow night, we'll see you next weekend. And, Allen, maybe in a few weeks, huh?" It was Sandra who spoke.

"Maybe." Allen's response was cool.

"Goodnight, little sis," Bob said kindly. Then he left with Sandra.

WHEN THE BLINDING CRYSTAL chandelier lights blinked back on, it startled both Allen and Julie. Maybe the limb hadn't broken the wires. Julie blew out the candle.

"Are you sure you don't want to stay here all night with Bob? It's awfully late to drive home to Oak Grove all alone."

Allen's face was blank. "No. No, I'll be okay. I'll make it fine."

Unwilling tears filled her eyes just before she headed toward her bedroom. He grabbed her by the bedroom door.

"Julie, listen to me—don't cry!"

Still turned away from him, she covered her face with her hands.

"Julie!"

Suddenly she brushed her hair from her temples and spun around. "Allen!" It was almost a rebuke that flashed from her tearless face.

"Julie?"

"Allen..."

"Snowdrift!" He laughed loudly.

Wordlessly, she brushed past him to the hall closet. Retrieving his coat, she placed it on his arm.

"Thank you for your hospitality," he said as he pulled his arms into the sleeves and straightened the collar. "Tell Bob and Sandra thanks, too."

As he opened the door, the chill dampness rushed in. "Maybe I'll see you at La Paloma College next year, Julie; I don't know."

"Goodbye, Allen." *Goodbye, dear Allen—goodbye.*

The screen door slammed shut when Allen was halfway down the steps. Then the darkness enveloped the form she had once grown to love. In a moment she heard a car door open and shut, its sound echoing through the empty street. She snapped off the porch light. It *was* rather chilly, even though the rain had stopped. She shut the door.

And there was silence.

Chapter 8. Fourth of July (July 1964)

THE FOURTH OF JULY holiday weekend crept up on the little town of Riverdale as quickly as the summer mornings' warmth crept up on the sleeping girls.

"Come on, gals, rise and shine!" The masculine voice rang from the doorway.

At the sight of Bob, both Sandra and Julie grabbed for the blankets they were already under as they let out a weak squeal.

"You'd better hurry if we're going over to Oak Grove," Bob insisted. "It's almost eight—"

Julie was the first to jump from the bed. Oak Grove meant just one thing—Allen. Why else had Sandra stayed overnight except that they could get an early start?

Julie had quite forgotten her recent fears and doubts about Allen that she had expressed to Bob and Sandra. Sandra hoped to herself that her and Bob's influence on the younger couple would be a good one. After meeting at the Oak Grove church where Allen was home for the weekend, the four once again shared the familiar old happiness and Christian fellowship.

"I guess I'll see you tonight in Riverdale," Allen said when Bob and Sandra were ready to go.

Julie nodded. "Okay."

IT WAS ANOTHER DELIGHTFUL pool party. Dr. and Mrs. Donaldson were so nice to the youth in sharing their pool and even providing refreshments. Bob was thinking of the wonderful evening they had spent as he made his way home from Sandra's house. Allen and Julie seemed to have a great time despite that little quarrel they had had after church earlier today. Bob hoped it wouldn't spoil things for them; they already had enough odds against them....

"Well, wouldn't you know it?" Bob smiled to himself as he pulled his car over to the curb in front of Julie's house rather than behind Allen's car in the driveway. But the house was strangely cold as Bob went inside. Allen and Julie sat at the kitchen table, both with a half-eaten piece of cake and only a fleeting glance occasionally for each other.

Finally, Allen forced a chuckle. "Man to man, Bob," he said, "can I impose on you?"

Bob sensed Allen wanted to be alone with Julie just then. "Sure. But come on out and say goodnight before you go."

Out in his trailer, Bob wondered just what exactly could be going on. After what seemed like endless hours of inextricable curiosity, Bob heard violent sobbing. Peeping through the trailer blinds, he saw two silhouettes on the porch.

"Allen, don't leave me!" Julie was crying.

Allen seemed to say something, but Bob couldn't quite hear. "He just better have a good explanation for hurting my 'little sis,'" Bob said to himself as he turned from the window.

Presently there was a faint knock on the trailer door. Allen entered, slowly and silently. In the darkness, Bob wasn't sure if that was a tear in the corner of Allen's eye.

"Well, Bob," he mumbled, "Julie and I—w-we broke up."

Bob hardly knew what to say. "Y—you did?"

"She did it," Allen said. "She said we should call it quits, but I guess she really didn't want to. I—I guess it must have hurt her—" Allen broke down and sobbed at that point.

"Well, things like that do hurt, I guess," Bob replied quietly.

"Oh, Bob!" Allen sobbed, shaking his head. "I just didn't think it would happen! I was such a big fool to treat her that way. I—I—"

Bob placed his hand on Allen's trembling shoulder. "I'm so sorry," Bob sympathized. "I know, love is deep—"

"Bob?"

"Yes, Allen?"

"She—she told Sandra a-and you everything—didn't she?"

Bob nodded quietly. "We understand. We're praying for you both."

For a long while the two sat in the silent darkness, neither knowing what to say. Allen only knew he needed the understanding prayers of someone like Bob, and Bob knew he had to fill that need.

"Let's pray," Bob said quietly, at last. And the two knelt.

"BUT IT JUST CAN'T HAPPEN!" Sandra exclaimed when Bob broke the news to her.

"Well, honey, maybe it's best—"

"How can you *say* that, Bob Miller?" Sandra was insistent. "Look how long it's been—almost four years—nearly twice as long as we've been going together. Poor Julie—she must really be an emotional wreck! Wonder if she'll go back to Rafael—or Glen or Larry. Too bad Greg Schultz isn't coming back to La Paloma. 'Course, there's still Kurt and Bill. Hey, yeah, Bob! You're pretty chummy with Bill lately—get busy!"

The next few days were miserable for Julie. As she had always done after breaking up with a boyfriend, she made a trip to the beauty shop for a drastic haircut. Soon she tied her long flowing hair with a crimson ribbon and put it in an out-of-the-way corner of her dresser along with Allen's many letters. Even Bob, so very partial to long hair on a girl, had to admit that Julie's short, short hair was actually very cute.

Chapter 9. August Anguish (August 1964)

"WELL, JULIE, KNOTT'S Berry Farm was great, wasn't it?"

"Um!" Julie showed some enthusiasm for the first time in nearly a month. "And so was Bill. It sure was a ball double dating with you and Bob. You know, with burying myself in Western Civ the past few weeks, I had almost forgotten anything else existed in the world!"

Sandra was blissfully satisfied with her friend.

The August days were warm and long. Julie remained calm although everything her hopes and dreams and future had been built on during the past four years had, it seemed, crumbled and vanished. She had shed all her tears that Fourth of July night during the agony that had lasted far into the morning. Now she could even face Pastor and Mrs. Macintosh and unemotionally spend a day with them in Oak Grove.

"PLEASE COME HOME AS soon as you can, Julie." There was a strange note of fear in Mrs. Scott's voice. "Your grandpa—" She choked up.

"Yes, Momma, I'll be home right away. Now don't you worry." Julie placed the dorm hall phone's receiver on its hook. Julie mulled over many questions during the forty miles between La Paloma and Riverdale, and Julie was hardly aware of either the familiar passing scenery or the gas pedal.

"Hi, Julie, come on in. Daddy's here, too." It was her cousin Sue who greeted her. The house was strangely silent as the two girls entered. Gingerly they stepped unnoticed just inside the bedroom.

Uncle Jake, Dr. Donaldson, Momma—and Grandpa Philip—it all swirled into a blur as Julie swallowed hard. Seeing his hand outstretched to her, Julie rushed to Grandpa's bedside, unable to say a word.

"He had the stroke Friday." "Yes, his entire side is paralyzed." "The ambulance will be here in about a half hour, Lora." The ghostly voices were those of Momma, Dr. Donaldson, and Uncle Jake as their uncanny sounds came from the kitchen. Although Sue sat in the room with her, Julie saw nothing as she stroked the thin gray hair from her sleeping grandfather's face.

Numbly, she opened her history book back in the dormitory room that night. The critical final exam would be in just two days. Professor Mackey had assured her she could raise her B+ average to an A if the final's grade turned out to be good enough. Nearly panic-stricken, she thumbed through her scribbled class notes.

When the test was over, Julie breathed a sigh of sweet relief. Someone had just given her inside information that her score was one point higher than that of the only other A student in the class! But her smile soon faded when she saw the note that the student monitor left for her at the desk in the dorm.

"Please come to the hospital right away."

Julie's heart leaped to her throat. Never in her life had she seen anyone in a coma, much less someone she loved. She hardly saw Momma and Uncle Jake and cousin Sue.

"Grandpa," she whispered, frightened. But he made no reply.

BACK AT LA PALOMA, Julie packed and cleaned her dorm room. The hours drug by. She was barely aware of the night and next morning that passed. Suddenly she found herself surrounded by the sickening white of the hospital walls. Fleetingly, she thought of what Sandra had gone through with her mother a couple of years ago. "Oh, God," she cried, "don't let him die—please, don't let him die!"

Through her tears, she caught glimpses of Momma's tear-stained face and Uncle Jake's uncharacteristically worried countenance. Julie realized just how much Grandpa meant to all of them. Wandering up and down the antiseptic green corridors and through the massive moving elevators, Julie caught occasional sight of cousin Sue or Uncle Jake or Dr. Donaldson—or Momma. As she paced in and out of Grandpa's room, her heart throbbed with intuitive horror until she felt her whole being would explode.

"He's gone, Julie." Uncle Jake's words sent a shock of incredible pain through Julie's trembling body. She ran to the door but stopped. Momma mustn't know just yet. The door's hinges shrieked as a white-clad figure stepped in. At once the ceiling seemed to be under her feet and the floor above her head. She felt entangled in the tubes and instruments that didn't know their work was no longer needed. She touched Grandpa's lifeless hand and then broke into uncontrollable convulsions. How long she lay sobbing on his cold cheek, she did not know.

Julie's world was a dreadfully unreal nightmare. There were all the arrangements, the flowers, the relatives and friends—even Pastor Macintosh and Allen—and the funeral. But after the cold damp earth had claimed its prey, Julie sensed the fearful torment of the listless house and the strange silent sound of death and the meaning of life's detours. Night after night the confused girl lay awake listening to the emotional sobs of her grief-stricken mother, and morning after morning awakened in the early hours by the same unwelcome sound.

"Mrs. Scott reminds me of my Pops," Kurt told Bob and Sandra. "He's never been quite the same since Mother died, you know."

"I sure know what you mean," reassured Sandra.

Bob looked at them both. "Well, it's a good thing for 'little sis,'" he said, "that she has such understanding friends like you two."

Kurt smiled understandingly.

Chapter 10. A New Fall Semester (September 1964)

THE WEEKS BEFORE THE opening for the fall semester at La Paloma turned into days. "Well," breathed Sandra, setting down her bundles, "I think we've got about everything. Boy, I sure like our pink bedspreads, don't you?"

"Sure do." Julie busied herself with putting her shopping treasures away.

"I bet we can fix up our room to look like a little dollhouse!" Sandra, dreamy-eyed, fingered the soft pile rugs and satiny quilting of the spread. "Oh, Julie, it's going to be such a neat year! La Paloma accepted Bob for this school year! And Allen and Kurt and Bill—maybe Rafael, too—will be around. Just think—this time next year I'll be *married* and we'll both we elementary teachers, Bob and me."

"And just think," Julie reminded, "this time a year ago, it was just at this point that our plans for being roommates *last* year fell through."

Sandra whirled herself around and flopped on Julie's bed. "But things just can't go wrong *this* time! They just *can't*—can they?"

"Well, I hope not." Julie was casually quiet. "Although Momma *has* been talking about maybe renting a little house in the La Paloma Village."

"Oh!" Sandra groaned, realizing that such a move could mean the loss of her roommate.

"Allen's going to be living on the La Paloma campus, you know," Julie interjected calmly.

"Really!" Sandra's eyes opened wide. "This *will* prove to be an interesting year."

"Back to the subject," Julie went on, "I *have* considered staying out of school and working a year—"

"You can't!" Sandra sat up and looked at her hoped-for roommate. "Julie, honey, I'm sorry if I sound unkind. I know you should love your mother like you do—she needs a lot of love now. But—"

Julie was silent, not even hearing Sandra's words.

"Sandra—" Julie's voice quivered—"what if Allen 'talks'? What if he tells other guys at La Paloma—about what we did—at Rainbow Rock?"

Suddenly Sandra understood Julie's seriousness. "I don't know," she whispered. "Just—just pray that he doesn't."

SOMETIME LATER, BOB followed Sandra into the dorm room, both arms filled with boxes and bags. "Is this all, sweetheart?"

Sandra looked around. "I think so. Thanks so much, honey, for helping me move in."

"When's Julie coming?" Bob planted a kiss on Sandra's forehead.

"Oh, she moved in already. I think she's out with Kurt tonight. At the library."

"Hmm, what a pair," Bob chuckled. "Well, I guess I better be on my way. It's almost door-closing time. See you tomorrow, doll."

"Night-night." Sandra closed the door softly. Tomorrow! That was the big day—registering for classes, buying books, seeing about work, and fixing up the room. Boy, it seemed like only yesterday that she was registering for first grade. How simple that was compared to this, her junior year in college! She remembered her sixth-grade year when she and Julie had become such great pals. Then seventh and eighth—she shuddered and laughed at the same time to think about it. That was when Miss Delavin, the upper-grade teacher at the little two-room country school in Riverdale—the same school where Sandra might teach!—had labeled her and Julie "boy-crazy." Back then it was almost common knowledge that Sandra Lee and Julie Scott would "turn out bad."

Sandra closed the curtains. Well, next summer Miss Delavin would be at her wedding, would meet Bob, and would find out just how wrong she had been. But Julie—what would Miss Delavin say if she ever knew about *her*—and Allen? *We grew up together—how could this happen?* Sandra almost thought out loud. *We both had pigtails, we both played accordions.* Sandra let her head fall onto the new pillow as her mind searched for the answer. *We both fell in love. We both survived what they used to say about us. We did everything together. How can we be in such different worlds now? And just why was the prettier, supposedly more intelligent one of us unable to escape from fate?...*

LATER THAT NIGHT, JULIE made her way down the stairs and through the softly lighted, green-carpeted hallway. She yawned. When Kurt got wound up on a subject, it took a while to get him unwound. She and Kurt were really alike—so scientifically minded and businesslike, enjoying brain probing, and each very independent. It was neat to have a "good buddy" relationship without the romantic sentimentalism—and complications. *He'll probably take Greg's place in my life this year,* she mused as she opened the door to a darkened room where Sandra was sound asleep.

THE CALIFORNIA SUNRISE came much too soon for the excited but tired girls.

"What time did you get in last night?" Sandra brushed her tangled hair.

"You were asleep." Julie fluffed her pillow. "About 9:30."

"With Kurt, huh?" Sandra closed the bathroom door behind her.

"Um." Julie straightened the rug. "Going to breakfast?"

"Yeah." Sandra drew a deep breath as she peered out the window. "You know, I was just thinking how lucky we are—"

"Lucky?!" There was a trace of scorn in Julie's voice. "After what has happened to me this summer?"

"I know it's hard—about your grandfather and all," Sandra sympathized. "But, remember, I went through it two years ago with my mother. And you've still got your Momma and Uncle Jake and your cousin Sue."

"But there was Aunt Jenny, too, last spring. Grandpa Philip was retired, you know. I didn't inherit a fortune from any rich relatives. You'll have your Aunt Hazel's estate and all your mother's things and won't have to worry a minute about school bills."

"Well, what about your California state scholarship—and the Rambler?"

"The Rambler—ha! That still belongs to Momma. She and Uncle Jake don't have that much stuff."

"What's money, anyway, compared to losing someone you love?"

"What's *anything* compared to losing someone you love?" Julie turned away. "I mean Allen, too."

"Oh, Julie, give yourself a chance!" Sandra touched her shoulder. "Maybe you haven't lost Allen—"

Julie only shook her head and pulled away to face the window. "I *have* lost love—the love of the most wonderful man in the world—but I have life," she said with finality— "a complete life of my own. A career girl—that'll be me—traveling, seeing the world, meeting and helping people. No strings at all, no ties to *anyone*—except God. Maybe I'll go into psychology, maybe music and the arts, maybe even computer science. Sandra, don't you realize—I'm free!"

Sandra said nothing as she tried to get a glimpse of Julie's world from where she stood in her own world—with Bob.

"Julie." Sandra swallowed hard to hide her nervousness. "W-we both have to go to register at 8:30, don't we?"

Julie turned slowly and handed the class schedule booklet to Sandra. She sighed softly and smiled. "Let's go," she said. "We'll be late for breakfast."

Chapter 11. Rendezvous

THIS WAS THE THIRD and final breakup of Julie and Allen. In just days, Julie Scott would meet Howard Davidson in advanced music theory class. He was an organ major who transferred to La Paloma College from Arizona State.

A month later, on the weekend of her 18th birthday, Julie would drive to a La Paloma weekend Bible conference in the mountains because she knew Howard would be there to play the piano. They inevitably fell in love and got into trouble a lot for PDA on campus. So they learned how to get off campus as much as possible.

After a year of dating, Julie and Howard got engaged; and the year after that they married and lived off campus while Julie finished her senior year, graduating from La Paloma College in 1967. Howard graduated the following year—1968—the first year that La Paloma changed from College to University status.

Sandra and Bob got married two months before Julie and Howard's wedding in 1966. Julie was Sandra's maid of honor, and Sandra was Julie's matron of honor. Rafael Gonzales and his sister Luisa sang at Julie and Howard's fairytale wedding.

Allen met and married Shirley, and they went off to create their own story.

THE FOLLOWING SHORT story is about Howard Davidson, the love of Julie's life whom she meets in the fall of 1964 during her sophomore year at La Paloma College. It is set in some future time after Howard's

graduation from college and his embarking on a concert artist career. Actually, it's a fantasy written by Julie Scott in 1967, during her first year of marriage to Howard Davidson.

THE KEYS JINGLED IN the dim foyer, along with the sound of approaching footsteps. In a moment, the massive oak doors creaked open. Mr. Howard Davidson, with his companion, stepped out into the bright sunshine. He gazed upward for a long moment at the majestic white stone building from where he had come. He could see the tall chamber that stretched toward the sky. He still pictured the great console inside.

"Tired?" The girl's voice struck the still air.

The man nodded slightly. "One more rehearsal day, Julie, and then..."

"A wonderful concert," she added, "by a marvelous artist."

He smiled, his eyes still fixed on the immense structure before him. "It's a fabulous organ." Together they started toward Howard's little red Volkswagen, which was almost lost in the late afternoon shadow of Carnegie Hall.

It was rush hour in New York City, yet Howard Davidson hardly saw the busy streets or heard the honking about him. His mind drifted back as he remembered how this had all begun.

It was in Phoenix—his own city. Even now, he sensed the breathless silence of the desert cathedral before his hands ever played a note. He felt the thrill of the keyboard as the sounds from the giant pipes filled the church and floated out into the summer night. But it hadn't stopped there. After San Francisco, there had been Dallas, and then—

"The Chicago concert," the girl's voice filtered into his reminiscence, "—how does that organ compare with this one?"

"Well, the Chicago organ had a better selection of reed stops, but this one has ten more ranks of pipes. However," he went on, "I've never seen such an acoustically responsive auditorium as—"

"Pardon me, Mr. Davidson," Julie broke in, "but we just passed the hotel."

With a chuckle, he turned the car at the next intersection. He still basked in the memories of the wild ovation in Miami and the fan letters from Los Angeles and Denver. And now—his biggest chance—he would perform in New York. Success here meant success of the entire concert tour.

"Thank you." Julie stepped out of the car when they pulled up to the front door.

"I must make a few more calls—president of the A.G.O., *New York Times* editor," he commented briefly. "See you later."

That night in the hotel, Howard stopped by the pay phone in the lobby. He unfolded the slip of paper that he drew from his pocket. "Call Janie—Cherry 4-9761," it read. After dialing with a slow, steady hand, he waited.

"Hello?" The woman's voice seemed unsuspecting.

"Hello. This is Howard Davidson calling. I received a message this morning to call—"

"Howard!" she cried in sheer delight. "How *are* you?"

"Fine, Janie." He smiled. "Never thought I would talk to you in New York City! Are you living here now?"

"No," she replied, "just vacationing. I just *happened* to see the announcement in the morning paper for your concert tomorrow night. They gave the name of your hotel, but I wasn't sure the message would get to you."

Howard chuckled. "Well, will I see you before we both leave town? You'll be at Carnegie tomorrow night?"

"You bet I will!" she assured him. "And if I can fight my way through the crowds—"

"I'll be looking for you, Janie." Howard pictured the scene.

"The French have a word for it, don't they?" Her voice was almost mysterious.

"Oh—*rendezvous*?" He chuckled. "Tomorrow night, Janie."

"Goodbye, Howard," she murmured, "until then."

Howard slept little that night. His music lay undisturbed on the desk close beside him, but Howard tossed and turned. Every hum of the elevator outside his room seemed to Howard like the surging wind past the huge shutters of the organ. Every onrush of traffic was a sudden *sforzando* of the 32-foot pedal notes. Every whisper of wind brought the ethereal flutes and strings from high above Howard's whirling brain. Every moonbeam was a great staff pushing the half notes, the quarter notes, the dotted eighths and sixteenths that filled his weary body.

Morning came at last. Howard was already in the parking lot when he realized Julie was not with him. Then he saw her slight frame leaning on his car.

"You're late," she said politely. "Weren't we to leave at nine?"

"I'm sorry." He hung his head. Then, "Hey, what are you doing out *here*? I mean, why did you come out—"

Julie laughed. "I knew you were deep in contemplation," she said. "You *have* been for several days. Anyway, it was such a lovely morning for a walk. So I just ended it here."

He opened her door. "I'm so glad you understand."

With a click, he snapped open his briefcase. "Check the music, will you, please?"

"Yes, sir!" Methodically, Julie lifted the stacks of music from the tan leather bag and, with secretarial efficiency, soon had everything in complete order. "Relax!" she commanded gently, looking at his tensed physique. "You know it all so well."

He took a deep breath as one hand fell from the steering wheel to shift gears. "Just the *thought* of tonight!" he stared straight ahead. "Julie, do you realize what it can mean to a musician's career!"

"Yes," she replied softly, "I know."

The empty auditorium was almost cold that July morning as Howard's skilled hands and feet called forth the powers of the greatest masters that had ever lived—Bach, Buxtehude, Franck. Although she had heard his repertoire many times, Julie stood wide-eyed and entranced, never moving a muscle except to turn the pages as Howard had beckoned. After all, that's what she was there to do.

Hour after hour passed. Boellman. Handel. Mozart. Sowerby. Hindemith. It was well past one o'clock that warm afternoon when Howard and Julie seated themselves in a small sidewalk café called *The Rendezvous*. The food was excellent, but Howard ate very little.

At long last he spoke. "The Organ Concerto in E-flat," he said dreamily as Julie nodded slightly. "How would it sound with the orchestra parts on a Steinway or Yamaha grand?"

She looked at him with almost amused curiosity. "Might sound all right. Probably sound *better* with an orchestra."

His deep blue eyes pierced through her seemingly complacent countenance. "But we *could* work it up in a few months' time—don't you think?"

"Could be, perhaps," Julie agreed. Then, with a twinkle, "You can't afford an orchestra, Mr. Davidson?"

"And you, *too*?" He smiled condescendingly.

There was a long moment of silence. The neon sign above the café, visible from their table, kept flashing on and off. *Rendezvous. Rendezvous.*

"Tonight!" Howard breathed half out loud. His gaze shot far past the milling crowds. "Just thinking of—of the future," he mused, "and all it could mean."

During the rest of the afternoon, Howard tried to relax as much as possible, but it was difficult in view of the big event that every moment brought closer and closer. He stretched out on a lounge by the pool and buried himself in the latest issues of *The Organ Journal* Julie had so thoughtfully brought. It was a lazy day, but he seemed to absorb little of the casual atmosphere that surrounded him. For a fleeting moment he thought of his pupils in California—those ambitious young organ students, so promising but so untrained as he once had been. He even thought once of visiting the museum at Carnegie—the Music Hall of Fame. At last, he dozed—his contorted body started to unwind—as the sun sank lower in the sultry sky.

Presently Julie appeared with a cool glass of lemonade. "Supper will be served in half an hour," she announced.

He looked blankly for a long moment into her innocent brown eyes. "Thank you," he said.

By seven-thirty nearly three-quarters of the auditorium was filled. It was not the first time Howard had seen so many people. He didn't even pace back and forth in his dressing room this time. Calmly, he stood to answer the faint knock on his door.

"Julie!" He spoke in mild rebuke.

"They're waiting for you," she said. "The music is ready, Prof."

Her adoring look made him swell with well-earned pride. "You're a great page turner," he whispered as he rushed past her onto the open stage where an explosion of applause awaited him.

Julie, dressed in black satin, was barely visible behind the great organ and tuxedo-clad artist except as her functional hand reached out to turn a page. Magnificent was the music that poured forth from Howard's hands and feet and heart! Like the roar of a thunderstorm, like the ethereal depths of an exotic sea, like the quiet charm of a Gothic cathedral—Howard gave all this, and more, to the spellbound audience. The time passed quickly, and the response was tremendous. Women threw flowers; the men cheered. They all gave him a standing ovation as Howard came back for bow after bow and encore after encore. Julie, almost misty, had taken the briefcase of music and headed backstage.

Howard grew tired as he signed autograph after autograph. It was a long time before the crowd of eager fans thinned out. Even the appearance of the heavy-set, stern-faced custodian who stood close by the organ with folded arms seemed to have little effect on dispersing the crowd.

As the tower clock in the distance was striking the hour, Howard turned to leave. It was then that he saw her. He peered through the dimly lighted hall until she was close enough to speak.

"Janie! You came."

"Yes, Howard. I said I would." With a white-gloved hand, she gave him her program to sign. "You were absolutely terrific!"

He smiled humbly as his trembling hand grasped the pen. Slowly, he handed it back to her as their eyes met for the first time in many years. He could see how the city light that diffused through a high rose window fell on her golden hair. "Janie," he said at last, "it's been so long."

She nodded. "I always knew you'd make good, Howard. I remember how it was in school—"

"Ah, yes." His mind drifted back across fond memories. He chuckled. "Remember how the kids always gave poor old Mr. Harris a bad time? Just because he was bald—"

She giggled. "Then there was the time we went with the class on that picnic. And guess who got lost!"

"Say, that was really when it all started, wasn't it?"

There was a silent pause.

Janie glanced absentmindedly at the now silent organ. "I'll never forget that banquet—and the music."

"Then there was the party at Larsons'—the very last one when—w-we thought we'd never see each other again."

"Tell me, Howard, you graduated from that university in California, didn't you?"

"Just a couple of years ago," he answered sheepishly. "I had a rough go of it at first."

"But you've got what it takes—determination *and* talent. I always admired that, Howard."

"And you, Janie, you were working for Dr. Hutchins in Ludington when I saw you last. Did you finish at Michigan State? I remember the big plans we used to talk about—"

"I did," she replied, "just a few years after—after we said goodbye. But I'm teaching now—in Ludington."

"Teaching! Janie, I'm proud of you."

"I'm proud of *you,* Howard. You know that. From the first day we stayed after school and I listened to you play the little spinet in the Ludington Cafeteria—"

Just then a toddler's exclamation echoed through the stillness. "There she is, Daddy!" And a tall, dark stranger stepped out of the shadows with a curly headed little girl in his arms.

"Honey, this is Mr. Davidson, the organist," Janie said as she took the wriggling bundle into her own arms. "Howard, I'd like you to meet my husband, Floyd Wright, and our little Debbie."

As the two men shook hands and exchanged greetings, a door from the hallway opened and Howard spotted a familiar form. He grasped her hand. "And *this* is the girl I could never have gotten through the concert without! Julie, I'd like you to meet the Wrights—Floyd, Janie, and—"

"Debbie," Mr. Wright smiled. "Nice to meet you both."

"Next year," Janie inserted, "you two must include Ludington in your itinerary."

The man beside her nodded politely. "Best wishes, Mr. Davidson—and Julie!" Then he turned, with his wife and child, to leave.

"Janie Wright," Howard whispered in awe when the darkness had enveloped them.

"So—*that's* Janie!" Julie's voice was teasing.

"Yeah." Howard laughed with her. "She still remembered who I was."

"Hmm." Julie seemed unconcerned. "Say, the A.G.O. president talked to me—he couldn't get through to you for the people! Anyway, he already wants to know about next year. I told him you'd write when we get back to California. But what *about* next year, Howard?"

He slipped his arm around her and planted a kiss on her forehead. "Together!" he said deliberately. "You and me—piano *and* organ. There's the E-Flat Concerto for a start—"

"Oh, Howard!" She responded to his embrace. "Do you *really* think I can—we can—do it?"

"Darling,"—he squeezed her suddenly— "you're a pianist, remember?"

"But something this *big*—"

"Hey, we're a team now, don't forget." He stroked her hair lightly. "Besides, I love you *and* our music."

"We'll do it, sweetheart—together."

She closed her eyes and laid her head against his broad shoulder. "I'll never regret the day we became a team."

"Neither will I!" he sighed softly. "Come on, Mrs. Davidson, we've got a big day ahead—Carnegie Museum, lunch at *The Rendezvous*, and a long trip home."

Don't miss out!

Visit the website below and you can sign up to receive emails whenever Juliana Harvard publishes a new book. There's no charge and no obligation.

https://books2read.com/r/B-A-EPQM-HHHNB

BOOKS 2 READ

Connecting independent readers to independent writers.

Also by Juliana Harvard

It Happened in Riverdale
It Happened in Riverdale
November Rain
That Morgan Boy
Beach City Breakup
Escape From Fate
"Marvelous"
More Riverdale Stories

About the Author

Juliana Harvard's writing spans more than five decades, from her adolescence until well past midlife. It is reflective of her most emotional moments, sometimes of ecstasy and wonder, sometimes of sadness and pain, and other times of sweet melancholy and contentment beyond words.

DISCLAIMER: "These are works of fiction. Any similarities to persons and places are frequent, intentional, and occasionally brazen, but generally fragmentary, inconsistent, and disguised with fanciful invention."

–Stephen Minot, *Three Genres*